Y0-CAP-842

DISNEY · PIXAR

TOY STORY 2

∾ **BOOK TWO** ∾

Disney PRESS

New York · Los Angeles

"Hey, Woody! Ready to go to cowboy camp?" Andy shouted, bursting into his bedroom.

Woody was a cowboy doll. He was one of Andy's favorite toys. His other favorite was a space ranger named Buzz.

"Never tangle with the unstoppable duo of Woody and Buzz Lightyear," Andy cried, linking the toys' arms together.

Suddenly, there was a loud *RIIIP.*

Woody's shoulder had ripped open!

Andy's mom suggested fixing Woody on the way to camp, but Andy shook his head. "No, just leave him," he said.

Andy handed the cowboy to his mom, who put the doll on a shelf. Sheriff Woody wouldn't be going to cowboy camp after all.

A few days later, Andy's mom began to clean his room. She
was having a yard sale and wanted to get rid of Andy's old toys.

Andy's mom grabbed Wheezy the penguin and brought him
into the yard. Woody couldn't let her give his friend away!

Woody whistled for Andy's dog, Buster. Woody climbed
onto his back, and the two raced outside to save the penguin.

But Woody couldn't hold on with a broken arm. He fell off
Buster and was picked up by a strange man.

The man's name was Al. When no one was looking, he hid Woody in his coat. Then he hopped in his car and drove away. The other toys watched from the window. They had to save Woody!

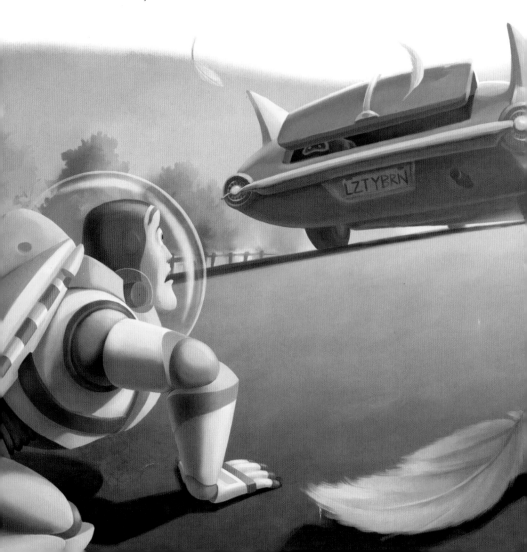

Al took Woody to his apartment. Suddenly, a packing crate burst open. Out popped a cowgirl named Jessie and a toy horse named Bullseye.

"Yee-haw! It's really you!" Jessie shouted.

Woody was confused. Why were the toys so happy to see him?

"Let's show him who he really is!" said an old prospector doll named Pete.

Jessie turned on an old TV show called *Woody's Roundup.*
Woody could hardly believe his eyes. He was the star!

Prospector Pete explained that the Roundup toys had
become valuable collectibles. Now that Pete had a Woody doll,
he was selling the whole set to a museum . . . in Japan!

Meanwhile, back at Andy's house, Buzz had figured out that Al was the owner of the local toy store. The toys set out at once to rescue their friend.

As the sun rose, they spotted Al's Toy Barn. It was on the other side of a busy road. The toys each picked up a traffic cone and dashed across the street.

Inside the Toy Barn, Buzz found an amazing display of new Buzz Lightyear toys. Each one was wearing a super utility pack.

As Buzz reached for the utility pack, a hand grabbed his wrist. It was a new Buzz Lightyear toy. The toy thought he had caught a rogue space ranger. He quickly tied Buzz to a box and placed him back on the shelf.

Meanwhile, the other toys had found Al's office. Listening to him on the phone, they realized that Al planned to sell Woody!

As the toys climbed into Al's briefcase, Buzz broke free. He followed his friends. But Buzz was being followed, too . . . by the evil Emperor Zurg!

Not far away, Woody's arm had been repaired. He looked brand-new. He was ready to go home to Andy.

"I belonged to a little girl once," said Jessie sadly. "She played with me every day, until she grew up. Then she gave me away. Even the greatest kids outgrow their toys."

Woody began to worry that Andy would forget about him, too. Maybe it was better to go to the museum.

As Woody and Jessie talked, the toys arrived at Al's apartment. Woody was confused. They had two Buzz Lightyears with them!

"There's no time to explain. Come on, Woody! Let's go," the real Buzz said. But to his amazement, Woody refused. What if his shoulder broke again? Would Andy still want him?

As the toys turned to leave, Woody watched a small, smiling boy on the TV. It made him realize how much he missed Andy.

"Hey, Buzz! Wait!" he shouted. He started to follow his friends, but the Prospector blocked the way. He had spent his whole life in a box, and he was ready for the museum.

At that moment, the toys heard footsteps. Al was coming!

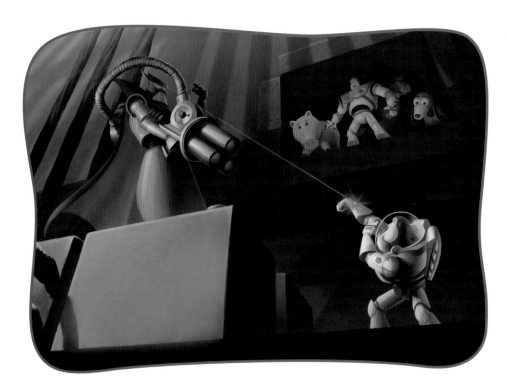

Al packed Woody and the other Roundup toys in a case and dashed out the door.

"We have to get Woody!" Buzz shouted. But as they headed for the elevator, they heard an evil laugh.

"It's Zurg!" gasped Rex.

Buzz and the new Buzz bravely fought off Zurg. Panicked, Rex closed his eyes and turned away. *Thwack!* His tail knocked Zurg over. Rex had defeated Zurg!

Al was getting away! Luckily, Mr. Potato Head spotted a pizza truck nearby. The toys jumped in and set off for the airport.

They found Woody at the check-in desk. As Al's bag thumped onto the conveyor belt, the toys jumped on beside it.

Thousands of boxes, bags, and suitcases swept past them, but Buzz kept his eye on Al's green case.

Buzz ran along the conveyor belt. Finally, he reached
Woody. But when he opened the bag, it was Prospector Pete
who popped out. *Pow!* He hit Buzz.

Buzz fought back. Soon he had tied the Prospector to a
passing backpack.

Meanwhile, Woody and Bullseye had managed to get out
of Al's bag. But Jessie was still trapped inside!

Woody jumped onto the plane. He searched the bags until he found Jessie.

Just then the plane began to move. Suddenly, Bullseye and Buzz appeared. Holding Jessie tightly, Woody dropped onto Bullseye's back. They were safe!